THE URBAN EROTICA
FAIRY TALE COLLECTION

Pied Piper's Pipe

THE URBAN EROTICA FAIRY TALE COLLECTION

Honey Cummings

4 Horsemen
Publications, Inc.

The Pied Piper's Pipe
Copyright © 2020 Honey Cummings. All rights reserved.

4 Horsemen
Publications, Inc.

4 Horsemen Publications, Inc.
1497 Main St. Suite 169
Dunedin, FL 34698
4horsemenpublications.com
info@4horsemenpublications.com

Cover & Typesetting by Battle Goddess Productions
Editor Vanessa Valiente

All rights to the work within are reserved to the author and publisher. No part of this publication may be reproduced, stored in a retrieval system, or transmitted in any form or by any means, electronic, mechanical, photocopying, recording, scanning, or otherwise, except as permitted under Section 107 or 108 of the 1976 International Copyright Act, without prior written permission except in brief quotations embodied in critical articles and reviews. Please contact either the Publisher or Author to gain permission.

This is a work of fiction. All characters, organizations, and events portrayed in this novel are either products of the author's imagination or are used fictitiously.

Paperback ISBN-13: 978-1-64450-085-9
Ebook ISBN-13: 978-1-64450-084-2

1

The Piper

Peter von Schmidt entered *Red's Bar*, relishing the air conditioning as sweat trickled down his temple from early summer heatwaves. Looking at his cell phone, the bar had barely been open an hour. With spring ending, it wouldn't be long before bikers came in droves, on their way into the bigger city for bike week. The worse of it was how they left a wake of unpaid tabs and broken pool sticks at every joint in a fifty-mile radius. This early, the bar was a ghost town, but it wouldn't be long before a cluster of bikers poured in, making a debacle of the weekly karaoke night.

They never bothered him. No one wanted to fuck with a guy who passed as a taller Stone Cold Steve Austin on a bad day. In fact, he had the real deal by about three inches standing at a height of six foot five inches. He often lifted weights, but that was to help him stay fit at the steel factory and the heavy loading of the machines and palettes. Scratching his goatee, he took a seat at the bartop, waiting for the time to pass.

His day had quickly gone downhill. He needed to keep a low profile.

"Hey Peter! You're here rather early." Red came out of the back office, her hips swinging in her jean skirt and red locks bouncing all around her shoulders. "In fact, a few hours early. Are you here for lunch?"

"Let me see the menu," he grumbled, rubbing the top of his bald head. "I have nothing better to do."

She reached over the cash register and pulled one free. "So, you going to tell me why you're at my bar so early today? I imagine it wasn't to watch me prep the ice trough for tonight."

He grabbed the menu. "I got laid off," he said, and her smile faltered. "Slow season is hitting, and they cut the crew in half today. Unfortunately, this year was my turn to get laid off."

"Ouch. I'm shocked no one else came with you." He stole a glance at her cleavage as she leaned over the counter. *If I didn't know better, she did that on purpose to brighten my day.* "Anything I can do to make you feel better?"

He sighed. "I'll live," he said, glancing over the menu. "Just get me a cheeseburger, add bacon."

"Ok, sweetheart." She punched his order into the touch screen. "Are you looking for a seasonal job? Or planning a long vacation?"

"I haven't made up my mind yet." Peter leaned back, enjoying the way Red's body dipped, in and out of her belly shirt. "Was thinking about leaving town for a while."

"Oh?" Her blue eyes peeked over her shoulder, gazing at him. "Heading south for warm beach weather? That's where I'd go if I were you. Some fun in the sun."

"Bah, too hot here as it is." Drumming his fingers on the bartop, he twisted his lips. "Was thinking north, way up north. Maybe Canada."

"Canada?" Twisting around, she arched into the counter, her breasts peaking above of her shirt and he realized she wasn't wearing a bra. "How about I give you a job here? Maybe change your mind about skipping town? Or delay it some."

Is she really flashing those at me? She's must be doing that on purpose and I ain't gonna look away. She's almost too big breasted to be playing that game.

"Oh?" He mimicked her sound, his eyes flowing up and lingering on her painted red lips. "What did you have in mind? Seems like someone doesn't want me to leave town just yet."

"Look, we both know those damn bikers are back and well, they almost put me out of business last year between unpaid tabs and repairs." She bit the tip of her finger, waiting for him to lock eyes before batting her lashes. "You think you can play my bouncer for a week? Until most of them leave town."

"How do you plan to pay me to stay then?" He arched an eyebrow, smirking at the sparkle in her eye. "What makes you think they'll pay their tabs this time?"

"You." She poked him in the chest, making his heart flutter as she bent down, revealing lacy red panties underneath her skirt. "There will be food and drinks on the house for you. That I can promise."

The Pied Piper's Pipe

"C'mon Red." He looked away, cursing his luck. *I can't afford a week without pay. She's outta her mind.* "I need cash for fuel. I'm headed north to find a summer job desperate for a strong-armed man to harvest, lift, or even sling asphalt before the mild weather ends."

"I could use some arms for heavy lifting," she said as she filled a large glass with cold beer, then setting it in front of him. "Please, Peter. Stay and I'll pay you with a favor."

Through the bubbly haze of yellow ale, her cleavage shimmered like gold. *What's the worse that happens? I get to fuck Red before I head out of town. Looks like the Pied Piper's back in business.*

"Fine," he drawled. "If not with cash, then with whatever I want?"

She perked up, her breast bouncing as she grinned. "Whatever you want."

2

Red's Tavern

B elly full, Peter took his time walking the entire parameter. As a customer, he hadn't really noticed there was more to the place other besides pool tables, stage, tables, and bar. The kitchen had all the basics and a walk-in refrigerator and freezer to match. He hadn't expected the dive bar to afford something that nice. Red spared no expense with timers, pressure cookers, and the works so her part-timer cook Chuckles could manage even a busy night solo. Granted, the poor kid was saving up for his own restaurant and even Gubering folks between part-time jobs. Out the back door he found the usual set of dumpsters, pile of milkcrates, and dirt parking lot where her old Wagoneer complete with wood paneling sat.

"Hey!" He shouted through the kitchen. "Should I park back here?"

"I would, makes it easier to leave and no worries that some drunk ass dented your car." Chuckles carried out a garbage bag. "If you get in over your head, let me know."

Peter snorted. "I got a good foot on you, and this ain't my first gig as a bouncer."

Chuckles laughed, slamming the dumpster lid shut. "With biceps as big as my head, I imagine no one fucks with you."

He followed Chuckles back inside. "Where the *hell* is Red?"

"Probably in her room." He flipped the fryer off. "Dammit, did she cook a hamburger on this?"

"Her room?" He walked to the push door.

"Through the office." Then, he shouted, "RED! Next time, clean the damn grill!"

Ignoring the flustered cook, he was back behind the bartop. The usual karaoke crowd was piling in at last, the host setting up and testing the equipment on the stage. He nodded at a few of his singing colleagues before pivoting into the next door. Inside the walls were lined with mismatched filing cabinets, an old computer, and a VCR humming as it recorded a four-panel, black-and-white security feed. *So that's how she knew I walked in.* Continuing to scan the room, he stopped at a far wall where a door lay cracked open.

Red released a frustrated whimper. Alarmed by the sound, he rushed across the office. Peter pushed through and froze. She was on her back, laying across an unkempt bed, her legs spread wide open, her hand diving under her lacy red panties. His eyes remained there as she continued to rub her pussy. At last he willed his eyes up, heart racing as he followed the divot over her belly button, up to where her other hand groped her bare breast, fingers twisting her nipple. She let out another hum, tilting her hips as she bit her bottom lip.

At last, they locked gazes, neither one willing to slow their fun.

"I'm sorry, I didn't..." *Dammit.* He couldn't seem to move his body, the sight of her arousal .... *I shouldn't be here. But...* "You look like you're having some trouble." *I've always wanted a chance to see more and boy, did I hit jackpot.*

She propped herself up, a smile blooming on her lips. "I can't lie, having you here, like this, sets my libido ablaze."

His face flushed, dropping his gaze. "Does that mean you have the hots for me, Red?"

"Yeah." She sucked the side of her cheek, her legs still provocatively spread wide open. "I've always wondered what it would take to fuck Peter von Schmidt."

He laughed, rubbing his bald head before glaring back at her. "You flatter me."

"So…" She arched an eyebrow high, scooting her crouch closer to the edge of the bed. "What will it be?"

"Seriously? You want to fuck now? Here?" Pulling the door shut behind him, he waited for her answer.

"Fuck me, right now." She wiggled out of her red panties, her toothy grin and hungry eyes making his cock throb. "Here, I'll even get rid of the last obstacle. I'm already wet thinking about it today."

He grunted, his hardon pressing against his jeans made him ache. She lifted the jean skirt, giving him a clear view of her shaven pussy. *How can I say no to that?* Yanking his shirt off, he took two long strides across the room as he unbuttoned his jeans. Before he could bend down to her, red painted fingernails were clawing to unzip him, and his hard cock throbbing in her hands. Her lips wrapped around his dick and began to suck. He reached out, bracing against the wall.

Someone's a hungry girl. Good gravy! Glad this was a twin sized bed, or I would have fallen...

He moaned. He was too long, too large to fit all the way into her mouth. The tip pressed hard against the back of her throat and she sucked, tongue wiggling. Looking down to her, blue eyes peeked up making sure he watched as she gobbled up his cock. She began pulling his dick in and out, the tip pressing firm against her lips before sucked hard until he slammed into the back of her throat again and again. He released another moan.

"Keep that up and I'm going to come," he warned, suppressing the orgasm daring to prematurely ruin his fun.

With a pop, she freed his dick from her lips. "Do you have a condom? If not, I have a spare."

He laughed, fingers dipping into a back pocket for his wallet. Flipping it open, he pulled out the wrapper. She plucked it from his fingers, tore it opened, then rolled the condom over his cock. Another chuckle came out of him as he marveled over how voracious her want for his dick seemed.

If only every time was this—wild and lustful, I would never stop masturbating.

Again, Red laid back and groped her breast. Legs opened wide as her finger dipped between the pink folds of her pussy, demonstrating how much the idea of having him inside her made her wet. Peter inhaled deep and held it. The problem wasn't her, but the bed was too damn low to the ground. With a finger, he motioned for her to flip it around and get on all fours to make this more comfortable for them both.

"You're too tall." She pouted.

"I have to be on my feet tonight, let's not wear out my knees just yet." His hand slid up her thighs, lifting her skirt above her ass. "Mmm-mmm!"

She wiggled her ass. "Like what you see?"

"Definitely." He rubbed his length against the opening of her pussy and swollen clit. "You think you can handle something this long?"

"I've dreamed about it long enough." She reached under, holding his dick against her as she rocked against him.

Humming from her heat, he couldn't stand it anymore. Pressing the tip against her opening, he slid inside her slow. She rocked back, her ass against his hip. With a knee, he made her spread her legs and the rest of his dick slipped in, their bodies snug against one another. She tightened around his cock and he throbbed. Gripping her hips, he pulled out, watching his length come out wet and throbbing until the cap pulled free.

He loved waiting until she leaned back, breaking inside her, and riding all the way in and repeating it until at last, her agony was too much. He moaned as she grinded against him, enjoying how she felt, rubbing his shaft in every sweet spot. *She's such a good fit.* Tired of riding the edge of his orgasm, he throbbed inside her, and she moaned. *Good, she's nice and ready.*

Fingers gripping her sides, he quickened each thrust of his hip until he pounded her harder—*faster*. She screamed, arching as she clawed at her covers. The bed knocked into the wall; *bang-bang-bang*. A deep inhale silenced her shrieks and her body shuddered. Her pussy wrapped tight around his cock and with the last hard shove, he peaked as well.

Throbbing as he came, he slowed his rocking, letting the pleasure of her orgasm coalesce with his own, until both of them hummed.

Several bangs thundered through the wall.

SHIT. Peter paled, his orgasm receding. *That's the kitchen!*

"Fucking Chuckles." Her head sunk into defeat.

Peter pulled out, chucking his condom into a nearby trashcan. "Dammit. I didn't think the walls were *that* thin."

She rolled over, flinging an arm over her face. "It's not the first time."

Peter's heart skipped a beat. *Why the hell does that make me jealous already?*

"Granted, it's been a *long* while," she said as she gauged Peter's reaction. "Thank you, I needed a good release."

"You're welcome... I think." He twisted, grabbing his shirt from the floor. "It's been a while since my last hooked up."

"Wasn't that when that Randi-chick came to town?" She pushed her breasts back into her shirt.

Peter's face flushed again as he tucked himself away. "Y-yeah. She caught me off guard, but it wasn't anything serious."

"Oh?" Red slid on her panties.

He smirked. "When was your last time? Since we're swapping stories."

Her face paled. "I didn't get his name."

Peter blinked, her face turning bright red now as she looked him in the eye.

"I went to some crazy masquerade orgy in the 'burbs." Standing, she straightened her skirt out. "No names, all masks, and so... like a true Red Riding Hood; I fucked the Big Bad Wolf."

"An orgy? In this small town?" He opened the door, motioning her through. *Good gravy.* "Did this town always sex craved?"

3

The Pipes

As they left the office, Chuckles was tending to the customers' drink orders. He gave a side glance at Peter before laughing and shaking his head. Whether the other eyes knew what the two of them had done back there was a mystery. He walked around, greeting the other karaoke singers, including Justin, the host.

The stage was set, fog machine rolling into a sea of colorful lights.

The bar was silent as the jukebox was muted, the reigns of entertainment handed over for the weekly event. As always, the cheesy introduction and hype was geared for a far larger crowd than the twelve patrons who barely filled the bartop and two tables.

"Welcome to another Thursday night of Justin-Time-Karaoke!" There was a collective moan in the bar, but it didn't faze the host. "Be sure to grab up the folders and see our collection. If there's a song you want that's not listed, just come see me! First up, let's have Peter up on stage! Singing, It's A Great Day to Be Alive by Travis Tritt."

Oof! I forgot I open with this song and today it's hitting me hard. I got laid and laid off.

The crowd built into a slow, awkward clap as he climbed on stage, grabbing the microphone from Justin. He disregarded the old prompter screen, having sung the song for so long it seemed as if it were a part of him. A foot tapped with the beat, his voice rumbling through and the bar fell instantly silent. If he hadn't been so bald, someone could have mistaken him for the real deal on stage. He picked songs based on the tone and gruff of his voice and he loved how he captivated a room.

One of these days, I just might run off and join a southern rock band. Ha!

In the trance of his performance, he hadn't noticed the bikers enter the bar. The only blessing was instead of the usual cacophony of laughter and cursing, they came in enamored by the big boy on stage singing better than the jukebox could have played. As Peter rumbled the last line and the music faded the leather vested crowd whistled and shouted.

"DAMN! The pipes on that man!" The tallest biker whistled again, gesturing to his crew to join him. "You sing some more like that brother, and old Tex will have to start throwing you some greenbacks instead of the jukebox for a change."

"I'll take your money any day." Peter smirked as he cut across the bar. *So, this is the crew she's worried about.*

"You leavin' already?" The big biker with TEXAS stitched on his vest scratched his beard. "Aw, don't leave so soon. At least give us another song."

"Don't you worry," Peter grumbled, marching pass the group. "My seat is just right here, near the door, just in case anyone decides to get too rowdy tonight."

"The bouncer?" He gave a toothy grin, then turned his attention to Red standing behind the bar. "You got yourself a bouncer this year, huh?"

"Had to. Last year you and your so-called crew nearly put me out of business." She didn't even make eye contact as she mixed a drink and popped open three bottles of beer. "You want your usual bucket of Coors Light or something with more kick to start off the night."

"Fuck yeah I want my beer and give me a Jagger Bomb!" He swung around in a grand gesture. "Get everyone here a Jagger Bomb."

Red stopped, placing her hands on her hips. "Not without a card. No one's getting shit."

"Aww c'mon, Ginger." He purred, pulling out a wallet with its chain clanking with each step. "Don't be so mean about it."

He slapped the card down and when she reached for it, he slid it out of reach. "I'm in no mood for your flirting. Why don't you sign up on Sinder and get yourself a one-night stand, instead of hounding me like a bitch in heat, Tex."

He released a long whistle. "Damn, girl. Someone needs to get laid."

Coming out of the kitchen swinging doors, Chuckles overheard the comment and choked on his drink, ducking back into the kitchen. Red's face flushed, cheeks puffing out. Peter watched her lips, wondering if she would retort or confess that he had just taken her on all fours barely an hour ago. Nothing. She lashed out again, sliding the card and turned to the register.

"You still want to buy the whole bar shots?" Her tone was every bit of a disgruntled mother's tone when one spoke to a child who had thrown a tantrum.

"N-no." He spun to the bar. "Sorry y'all! I ain't that rich. Perhaps another night!"

The bar filled with groans and laughter. His biker pals were disappointed, but the karaoke regulars sniggered knowing full well what to expect if this was going down like last year. Many had paid for the unwanted drinks to make up the difference, or at least lighten the blow to Red's expenses.

"A Jagger bomb and a bucket, right?" She slid the card.

"Yeah, that'll be good to start with." Tex drummed his fingers on the bar, his smile vanished. "I'll give that Sinder thing a try. So, when did it become mandatory to pay up front?"

"New policy." Red pointed above her head to a sign, pay as you drink, or water from the sink.

"You're just ruining my fun. Can't a guy just open a tab?" He groaned, pulling at his beard.

He pointed to another sign, reading: no open tabs. Pay as you go. "Thanks to you, this is the normal night of fun."

When the receipt finally printed, she slid it, along with a pen and his credit card, in front of him. "Damn. What bullshit. I'm a regular."

"You're seasonal," she amended, nodding at the karaoke crew. "They're my regulars.

Coming here one month each year doesn't make you a regular."

"All right, all right. Can we get a pool table for an hour or two?" He gave her a smug look.

She mirrored the goofy grin. "$50 for the first two hours."

"Dammit, woman!" He threw up his arms. "Fred, pay for your damn pool table!"

A skinny twig of a biker appeared. He grinned at her, his teeth green a few already missing.

Peter cringed, but Red remained unphased.

The biker dropped a fifty on the counter, and she pulled out a tray with balls, chalk, and a rack. He took them and a group by the pool table roared to life, drowning out the karaoke. Peter snorted, frustrated that he couldn't hear Wendy nor old Sam sing over the clacking of pool balls and barking bikers. Red came around the bartop, her swaying hips making him shudder as she dropped off and picked up beers from all over the place. For one cook and one bartender, she kept drinks filled, food coming, and tabs ready.

At last she came in his direction and he straightened himself. She flicked her hair back over her shoulder and placed an icy mug of water on his tiny table. The heat of her hand on his shoulder made him think of how those red lips wrapped around his cock, his blood rushing at the thought there might be a second round later. Her breath tickled at his ear, whispering just loud enough to make it clear through the music and bikers.

"Are you ok over here?" Her other hand rested on his knee, making his groin ache to feel her gentle touch.

"I'm fine. Just pissed I can't hear over these assholes." Tex was giving them the stink eye as he leaned on his pool stick. "You handled him like a champ, I'm impressed."

She laughed, her hair slipping off her shoulder to rest on his. "You learn to take no shit in my line of work."

"Well, I hope to make it smoother tonight." Her hand slid up his inner thigh, squeezing until he grunted. *Good gravy, she's making me hard again.*

"It's your turn." She breathed.

He paled. "My turn?"

"Your turn," she echoed, rubbing her warm hand across the crotch of his jeans before pulling away. "Justin's calling you to the stage, sweetheart."

FUCK! She meant for karaoke. He took a gulp of ice water, then marched towards the stage.

The Pied Piper's Pipe

The only relief is he hadn't gotten completely hard, otherwise he'd have to cook up some excuse. Chuckles came out from the kitchen and started helping her cater to the demanding bikers, both registers dinging. He managed to get to the stage and realized he hadn't put in for a song number two.

"What am I singing?" He cracked his neck, waiting for Justin to select a song.

With a sparkle in his eye, he gave a devilish grin. "Mustang Sally."

"Of course." Peter sighed, leaning into the microphone stand.

Again, the music started, his heel tapping to the beat as he sang the lyrics. In an instant, the bar went silent once more, and he couldn't stop smiling. Screeching the chorus, he locked eyes with Red and she laughed. It started to feel like a secret conversation, and she snapped her fingers, dancing as he howled on. The song ended and he felt cheated out of the fun of stealing glances across the bar at one another. Whistles and claps came from the pool tables and his grin faltered.

"One more song." He leaned over to Justin. "Let's do another Tritt song."

"I know just the one to match the atmosphere." Justin was pulling it up on the system.

The name appeared on the prompter, and he smirked. "This song is for the biggest troublemaker in the joint, Red."

The music started and everyone whistled and howled. Peter winked at Red, pointing at her as he sang. Fast-paced, he roared the lyrics to T-R-O-U-B-L-E with practiced ease and the whole bar was signing along by the end. Feeling satisfied, he left the stage laughing and thanking the karaoke peers for their compliments. He ignored the bikers and their kudos, intending to march towards the table when Tex's landed a heavy hand on his shoulder.

Peter stopped, twisting to look down at him as every muscle tensed in his bulging arm and heaving chest, forcing his shirt to stretch across his pecs.

"Down boy!" Tex threw his hands up in surrender. "Can I buy you a beer?"

"Why?" Peter returned to his table, gulping down the rest of his water.

"Those pipes. Man, you ever think about singing for a band. I know one looking for a singer like you." Tex waved off his turn at the pool table, handing the pool stick to one of the biker chicks who had come in with them. "Seriously, I bet you could go places."

"I only sing for fun." Sitting down, he locked eyes with Red who frowned seeing Tex talking to him. "Look, I'm working as the bouncer here. Perfectly content with that."

"Well, if you get tired of the grouchy Ginger over there, just hit me up." He slid his cell number on a business card to Peter, and he crushed it in his pocket.

Tex turned back to his crew, but before he could speak the cracking of a pool stick brought everything to a screeching halt. Peter jolted to his feet, blood rushing. Two bikers were screaming into each other's faces, shoving into one another like two raging bulls. A girl was crying, covering her face. Most of the crew were already shitfaced, so they all watched the events unfold in a stupor.

"YOU FUCKING PUT YOUR HAND UP MY GIRL'S SKIRT!" roared the one carrying the broken pool stick. "I WILL CAVE YOUR HEAD IN!"

He raised an arm high, the bulk of bikers pulling the offender away. Peter gripped the wrist hard, wrenching it until the pool stick bounced against the floor. Before the other arm could swing, it too found itself dropping the impromptu weapon and twisted behind him.

"LET ME GO!"

"Don't think so. You're done." Peter shoved him around the pool table and outside with insane ease.

I've lifted steel bars with more bite than this guy.

The bikers followed, none of them challenging Peter. Letting go, the man fumbled forward, pale from the ease he had been dealt with and pulled out of the bar. The girl sobbed, her words belligerent other than his name, Fred, as Peter glared with pure rage.

Tex nodded. "Let's call it a night, boys. We got business to discuss about Fred, anyhow." He motioned a goodbye as he straddled a white Harley Davidson Road King. "Sorry for the trouble. I'm glad she finally has some muscle."

4

Closing Time

Marching back through the door, Red was tabbing out the regulars. Peter returned to the pool table, grabbing the broken stick, then gathering the pool balls into the tray. The music had ended, karaoke disrupted and the lights flickering on. She's closing down early. That's not like her. I've seen barfights here, cops and all, but she's never just shut the place down over a scuffle.

He waved farewell to the karaoke crew and helped Justin load his equipment. Silence held strong between him and the patrons as they cleared the parking lot. Walking through the front door, he reached for his empty glass to find it gone. Daring to scan the bar for her, he met Red's gaze as she punched in the tips on the last of the tabs.

"Lock that door, would ya?" He did as she asked.

He sat at the bar and watched her. "You ok? Did I do something wrong?"

"No." She slid the receipts into the slot of the register. "Last time they argued like that, they nearly destroyed this place. I'd rather take a loss by closing early than deal with that shit."

The bedroom in the back flashed in his mind and his stomach knotted. "You live here."

"I do. Sold the house to pay for last year's bullshit. Haven't totally gotten back on my feet just yet." Peter hissed, he had no idea, but Red had always kept to herself. "We didn't do too bad. It helped making those dicks pay as they go."

"Well that's an improvement." A motorcycle rumbled pass on the highway and they both froze, glaring at the front door. "Look, I'll stay until we're both confident that they won't return."

Her brow folded and at last, she looked him in the eyes. "I'd like that. Thank you."

His brow lowered, his voice turning stern. "Did they hurt you?"

"No." She snorted. "I was nowhere near the fight."

He shook his head. "I meant last year."

She froze, then finished locking the register. "No, but it scared the shit out of me." Her shoulders shook. "The cops took forever to get here, and I couldn't afford to hire them as security."

Peter leaned back, drumming his fingers. "Well, you got me this time. Those rats will have to answer to Peter von Schmidt, your personal Pied Piper."

She giggled. "Did you just call yourself the Pied Piper?"

Peter raised his eyebrows, then shrugged. "It's a nickname from work. Kind of grew on me."

Smirking, Red leaned on the bar, training his eyes to fall onto her cleavage. "And are your pipes that voice or something longer and stronger?"

His face flushed, and he scratched his goatee. "You know exactly how to make me blush, you know that, Red."

"It's cute." Pulling away she left him sitting there in silence as she went back into the kitchen.

In the back, he could hear the muffled conversation of her helping Chuckles clean up after a night of cooking. Red came out and sat a cold mug filled to the rim with Bud Light and basket of fries in front of him. Before he could even say a thank you, she winked and disappeared back through the kitchen door. The minutes dragged by, the clanging and sounds of the sink soon falling silent. The lights went out, and she came through the doors, drying her hands in an oversized rag. Flipping open the cooler, she grabbed a Corona, then a lime from the garnish box and slinked around the bartop and slid beside him.

"Your dragging around like an old lady." He smirked taking a sip of beer.

"I do feel old on night's like this." She sighed, squeezing the lime into the bottle. "Seemed like a good night to lend him a hand back there and give the kitchen a good scrub down."

"You keep this place pretty tidy." He gave her a side glance. "When I walked the parameter, trying to gather my bearings, I didn't notice any trash or dust on any surface."

The Pied Piper's Pipe

"Well, it's easier to maintain when I live here." She guzzled another long swig.

"So, you opened this joint all by your lonesome?" he asked, curious to know more about her backstory.

Setting the bottled down, she laughed, fingering the opening. "Well, I guess my ex-husband deserves some credit for opening this place. As for keeping it running for the last five years, that's all me." Another long pull on the Corona, she exhaled. "Tex is a good guy, but his biker gang almost costed me the bar last year."

"How can you call him a good guy if he almost destroyed the place?" Peter drained the last of his Bud Light and tossed it into the trash.

"Every month, he still sends me money to repay me for the damage."

"No shit." Peter blinked and watched as Red drained her beverage. "It can't be much though."

"No, but he's never been late since he started last year. I can't talk too much shit about him for that." Spinning in her chair, her hands pressed against atop his thighs as she leaned in closer. "Enough about those assholes. How about you let me play with your pipe once again, Mr. Pied Piper."

Peter laughed, averting his gaze as he blushed at the idea.

"C'mon." Her hands slid slow across his thighs, the heat of them searing through his jeans. "You can't say you weren't hoping for a second round."

Caving, he met her gaze and she batted her eyes. "If I didn't know better, this was never about hiring me to be your bouncer or helping a customer who was out of the job."

"You caught me," she breathed, fingers clawing at his button and zipper.

The Pied Piper's Pipe

"Were you planning to pay me in cash or..." He grunted, her fingers teasing his growing erection with practiced skill. "Blow jobs won't keep the lights on, Red."

She blew warm air against the tip and he throbbed in her hold. "You're right."

He braced an arm on the countertop and gripped the barstool under him. Last thing I need is to fall straight back. At least she's going slower this time. A shudder rocked him as she began stroking his cock with her hand, the other cupping his balls. Her nipples had grown hard against atop his thighs as she lean into his crotch. Lips tickled at the underbelly, kissing, and teasing their way from the tip and down the length of his pipe.

Red didn't stop at the base. Deepening her kisses, she suckled and licked his balls, making him moan. She paced herself, stroking his shaft as she made love to the tender sack making him grow harder with each lick. A nibble made him tighten as she denied his balls from toying with them. Her thumb slid to the tip of his dick, circling there, slick with precum as she pleasured her own clit.

She moaned, and he leaned forward, white knuckled as he fought the urge to speed the process.

Pulling off his balls, her blue eyes met his own with a wicked grin. And he throbbed with desire. The pleasure and arousal building at his core made his body feel boiling hot. Wet and soft, her tongue licked from the base to the tip. He moaned, and he closed his eyes, enjoying the primitive sensation of touch, pure and provocative. The tip of her togue teasing the opening of his penis before her lips slid slow and tight down his shaft.

She changed direction. A firm thumb stroked hard on the bottom half of his long cock as her lips slid to the top and back to meet the rising of her hand. She rolled his balls in her other hand, massaging soft and gentle, adding to the experience. He leaned harder on the counter and at last his hand broke loose from the stool. His fingers entwined with deep red locks, moaning as he pressed his dick deep into her throat, desire taking hold.

She moaned as she shifted, his cock riding across her tongue and connecting with the back of her mouth. She abandoned her play with his balls, leaning in and let him press her where it felt best. He rocked his hips, the stool creaking under his weight as it squeaked against the screws keeping it fastened to the wooden floors.

Thank you to whoever screwed these bad boys to the floor!

She released another moan, and she began sucking, her mouth tight on his throbbing erection. He began panting, fighting his rising orgasm close from exploding.

A little longer... this feels so damn good!

Thrusting in and out, he quickened his speed. Her nails dug into him as if hugging him into her. Slick and hungry, she took him in over and over. The tip of her tongue curled up, the hard nub riding the length of his shaft. And he lost it. Humming, he slowed his rocking as he came. She swallowed, twice more as he throbbed and released for the last time.

He freed her hair, trying to catch his breath. She sat up, a sparkle in her eyes as she licked her lips.

Good gravy. I don't think she's done.

5

Red Hot

Peter's brow arched high as he watched with erotic curiosity. Red removed her panties, then sat back down, hiking her skirt up. She was barefoot and he marveled to where she had ditched the cute sneakers in all the commotion.

She raised a leg and laid across his thigh, opening wide to show him her world.

That's what he meant by that in Crash into Me! Dammit, Dave Matthews Band!

Tugging her shirt over her bare breasts, she began to rub herself. Peter cursed the fact he was spent for a while before he could go another round. He could feel the heat of her stare as he grunted, balls tensing as her fingers rubbed her pussy. There wasn't a detail he didn't want etched into his memory as he took in every curve, every inch of flesh.

Her breasts were firm, her arousal from playing with his cock still driving her want for him. Nipples stood erect, a subtle brown against warm golden skin. He swallowed.

She tans in the nude. Maybe I should rethink my plans to head south if she wants to tag along.

His eyes widened as she groped her own breasts, raw and rough. The flesh of it bulged from between her fingers and again, he cursed the fact he wouldn't be able to get hard just yet. At last he dared to look higher at the glare he knew awaited him. Lips were caught in the grip of her teeth and blue eyes glossy.

She huffed a laugh. "I want you to watch me play with myself."

The Pied Piper's Pipe

He swallowed and let his gaze return to where her finger circled her clit. Her pussy swollen and wet, making him stroke himself, hoping to speed up his recovery time.

"Look how wet you make me."

Another grunt escaped him, some hope building as his dick throbbed under his touch.

"Having your cock in my mouth makes me want to touch myself." She shifted, his view of her pink folds making him throb once more. "Do you want to fuck me again?"

He inhaled deep. What a loaded question!

"You want back inside me?" Her fingers slid slow into her pussy, rubbing in and out.

Peter stroked himself in unison, and she began to moan. He was growing stiff once more, his dick dripping in anticipation of what he saw before him.

"Tell me, Peter." Her voice deepened, dripping with lust. "Tell me where you want to fuck me with that big dick of yours."

He sucked the side of his cheek, unable to look away as her fingers came out, wet, and began rubbing her clit once more. "I want..." Chills rattled him, cutting his words short.

In his peripheral, her lips curved into a wide grin. "Anything you want, you can have it all."

Stroking his cock, he wasn't hard enough to take her. He leaned forward, his lips latching onto her breast, and he circled her nipple with his tongue. She abandoned groping its match, pulling him into her chest so she could balance on the stool. His freehand slid up the inside of her thigh. Slick from her want, his fingers found the hot silk of her swollen folds.

Rubbing her opening, she didn't slow her circling of her bean as he suckled on her breast. He could feel her throb from his touch, and he slid two fingers inside her warmth, pushing knuckle deep. Her body tightened around him.

Twisting his wrist, her legs jittered. There's the sweet spot.

She whimpered, and he rubbed slow, letting her inhale deep and fall into the pleasure of it. Her circling of her clit faltered. He switched breasts, nibbling her nipple. Her pussy tightened on his fingers again and he ran with it. Stroking hard and fast, she grew more wet with each push and at last she shrieked.

Her arms flailed and gripped his shoulders, nails biting into his skin. Peter didn't slow. Her orgasm pulsed through her. Legs shook and she folded forward as a gush of fluid brought his stroking to a halt. He still rubbed himself, his erection still not where he needed it to be.

At last, they met eyes once more and laughed.

"I don't think I've ever hated not getting an instant hardon from a blow job in all my life," he confessed, staring at his dick's betrayal. "You let me down, buddy."

She pushed her shirt down, bringing her leg off him and pulling her skirt back in place. "Sorry, I'm rather brass in the moment."

"I can tell." His eyes widened, a chill rolling up his spine. "And I can't lie, it's super-hot."

Her face burned bright red, and she covered her face. "Please don't blab about my fetish."

"What fetish?" He gave her a baffled look.

"I like it when men watch me touch myself."

"I like watching you touch yourself." The words tumbled from his mouth before he could stop himself. "Wait, that didn't come out as sexy as I thought..."

The Pied Piper's Pipe

They jolted in their seats as a loud knock thundered from the kitchen, beating on the back door.

Peter furrowed his brow, tilting his head in a questioning manner. "Chuckles?"

She held her arms and shook her head. "No. He has a key. He would've texted me if he'd forgotten it."

Her eyes fell to her phone on the counter, and he looked to the kitchen door. "I didn't hear a motorcycle. Then again, I was a little distracted."

"Only cops and assholes knock on doors like that." She inhaled deep, holding it a moment before releasing it. "And cops knock on the front door."

Peter stood, tucking himself away and closing his pants. "I got this."

He started to walk away but she gripped his arm with both hands. "Peter. Be careful."

Winking, he marched through the kitchen and halted before the back door. All the locks were in place, a deadbolt, the lock on the knob, even a chain and slide bar. Red's front door had the same array. Another series of banging exploded on the door, and he flipped the light switches. The florescent lights overhead flickered to life and he prayed one of those switches lit up the backlot.

Whatever they did last year, it really shook her up good and someone's about to learn how hard a steel worker punches.

One by one, he started to unlatch the locks.

Another burst of banging. "OPEN THE FUCK UP, BITCH!"

The knob twisted, the last lock still in place.

The Pied Piper's Pipe

That's the dickwad who I tossed out front for breaking a pool stick! Oh, he's about to get a fucking fist-sandwich!

Peter threw open the door, locking on a black-eyed skinny biker. His vest gone, he looked like a wet noodle as Peter bowed up. He took a few strides forward and the man countered, stumbling back in alarm.

The door slammed shut behind Peter and the man cowered into the dumpster, falling into a stack of milkcrates as he gave a silent stutter.

"Fred, right?" Peter's voice rolled from him like a growl, his brow low.

"L-l-l-look man," His pubescent voice cracked as he pleaded with Peter, the angry giant, for mercy. "I didn't know she was your girl. I just wanted to scare her."

"Like you did last year?" A vein pulsed on Peter's forehead and neck, every muscle in his body drawing taut with the adrenaline.

"About that, no one knows I did that, and..."

Peter punched the dumpster beside Fred's head, denting the metal. He squealed like a little girl, his knees shaking as he pissed himself. Peter was unmoved as blood trickled in a singular line from a busted knuckle, the blood black against the green paint. Nostrils flaring like an angry bull only made Fred cover his head, waiting for the ass-whooping coming to him.

Reaching down, Peter grabbed him by the scruff like a street dog. A firm grip with a ball of shirt and the back of his pants, it took one hi-ho swing to launch Fred up and into the dumpster.

Satisfied with the result, he slammed the lid closed and marched for the back door.

Red waited there, her eyes wide at the speed in which he had addressed the man.

The Pied Piper's Pipe

"Your hand." She sidled to let him in before rushing to close and lock the door.

"This." His eyes looked to the busted knuckle and snorted. "I've done worse at work. Just needs ice."

"I'll grab something from the freezer." She rushed pass him.

6

T-R-O-U-B-L-E

Peter pulled out his phone and the crumbled paper with Tex's number.

[Peter: Come get your trash. Peter.]

The reply was fast.

[Tex: Fucking Fred. Where is he?]

[Peter: In the dumpster behind Red's Tavern.]

There was a long pause.

Red exited the walk-in freezer, a bag of frozen peas in hand. She gently placed it over his knuckles.

"Thank you," he muttered, still glaring at his phone.

With that, she spun, mumbling something about a "first aid kit" and "fucking Chuckles."

[Tex: We'll get him, and make sure he won't mess with her ever again.]

[Peter: Good. Next time he'll become a permanent shit stain in the parking lot.]

[Tex: If there's a next time, I'll help put him there.]

He smirked, his knuckle throbbing and aching. "Frozen peas are a smart idea."

"Don't eat them." She came in swinging her hips with the kit in hand. "I bought a few bags years ago just for this use only."

He glanced at the expiration. "Good gravy, these are older than my grandma."

Red laughed, the tension of the moment passing at last. "Thank you."

"I'm the bouncer," he replied, removing the peas so she could bandage his hand.

She sighed. "Not for that," she said. After taping the gauze, she met his gaze. "Thank you for making me laugh."

Rubbing his bald head, she averted his eyes. "Life's too short not to find humor in the small things."

She put the leftover items in the kit and closed it, leaving it behind. With a come-hither finger motion, he abandoned his bag of peas and followed her out of the kitchen. As she rounded the bar, she wiggled out of her skirt, leaving it on the floor. With a playful pirouette, she pulled her shirt up and off.

At last, she was completely nude. Between the passing time and adrenaline rush, Peter's pipe was back in business. Pacing himself, he followed her across the building where she waited at the pool table. He too mimicked her shedding of clothes, kicking off his boots, pulling his shirt off, and freeing his erection as he shuffled off his jeans. Peter closed the gap between them, stroking his cock.

"Do you think the pool table's high enough to prop me into a more comfortable position?" She smirked.

"Oh yeah." His dick throbbed, gauging the height. "I take it we're picking up where we left off?"

"Unless your knuckle hurts too much."

He laughed, rubbing his bald head with his freehand. "I think I'll manage it just fine."

Red pulled herself up on the pool table. Her legs spread open before him and his eyes fell once more to her pussy. Both of her hands slid down, spreading open her folds like the petals of a pink rose. A single finger slid slow and with great purpose inside. There was an agonizing pause before she drew her figure up and began playing with her clit.

He stepped closer, his eyes locking on the prize. She grew more wet with each passing moment. He timed his rubbing with the slow circling, reaching his tip as the finger rolled over the top and stroking down as it fell. Another step forward and at last he could trail his fingers from her knee to her thigh. Greedy, her fingers dove into her pussy and it made him moan with the desire to be inside her.

Changing tactics, he abandoned his cock and slid his fingers up her stomach until he cupped her breasts. He licked one nipple than the other. She hummed, and he continued his climb fully aware of how desperate her fingers spun and dipped into her pussy. Hands slid over the breasts until they framed her jaw. Pressing his lips against hers, he kissed her deeply.

The Pied Piper's Pipe

A shudder rolled over him as they moaned into each other's mouths. Tongues tangled, pulling, and pushing as if in a struggle to decipher who tasted better than the other. His cock rubbed against her thigh until the tip pressed into the back of her hand. Sliding an arm behind her, he coaxed her to lay down. She yielded, lowering, and stretching her body before him. Her hands pulled away, reluctant to abandon their play so soon.

Peter straightened, his hands raking down her body until he could lean back and see all of her. His hard cock rubbed against her wet pussy, teasing her one last time. Her hands reached down, and he grabbed her wrists. Pinning them above her head, she grinned in reply. His cock slid inside, hard and fast. She arched, a gasp then shriek escaping her. He moaned, the tight heat making him throb inside her.

Satisfied, he had pressed as far as he could, he let go of her arms. Bracing himself on the pool table, he rocked his hips, pulling and pushing. Her knees rose high, hugging his torso and he could rock deeper into her. He loved how she bit her lip, staring him in the eye, never looking away. When she started to slide away, he grabbed her thighs and pulled her back to the edge of the table, pressing himself against her.

"You like playing with yourself but..." He licked his lips.

"But?" she grinded against him, her pussy matching the motion with waves of tightening.

"Do you like it..." His words lingered.

"Like it."

His hand glided over her hip, his thumb pressing against her swollen clit. Circling, he felt her spasm around his cock. She inhaled deep, arching as he rolled over the tender nub. Her legs shook where they hugged into him, knees digging into his ribs. The heat of her arousal waved from her and he started to rock his hip again. She whimpered, tilting her head back, eyes shut. Hands reached up, clawing at his arms, unable to pull him free.

Pressing firmer, thumb slick from her pussy, each pull drawing more, making each push quicker than the last. She tightened, moaning louder. The arch of her body higher. He had her peaking. Abandoning her clit, he wrapped his arms around her body, pulling her against him. The fever of their passion pressed into one another as her grind against her, deep and fast.

Fingernails scratched down his back and he fought the urge to peak. Not yet, I want more. She's so wet and…

A howl escaped her before she bit into his chest to ride it out. He pressed hard and stopped inside her, enjoying the pulsing of her pussy as she rode out her orgasm. She melted, muscles relaxing as she let herself lean back into his arms, panting.

"Dammit," he muttered.

Swallowing, she caught her breath. "What's wrong?"

"I don't have any condoms," he confessed, pulling away. "We used the only one I had. Where do you keep..."

Before he could walk off, she grabbed his arm. "I've got a naughty proposal."

He lifted an eyebrow at her. "You plan on swallowing again?"

I'm down for another epic blow job.

"That or..." She slid off the table and twisted around, bending over in a provocative pose spreading her ass cheeks open. "Or you can try something a little tighter?"

"But don't we need..."

She reached into the corner pocket and grabbed a bottle of lube. "I have it right here."

The Pied Piper's Pipe

"Good gravy!" He rubbed his head, shaking his head in disbelief. "You had this whole night planned, didn't you?"

"Honestly, I was jealous of you hooking up with that out-of-towner, Randi." She sat the bottle beside her, wiggling her ass once more. "Well, Mr. Pied Piper, which is it? Blow job or this?"

Snorting, he snatched the lube up and squirted some on his fingers. "Please tell me this isn't your first time."

"Not the first time," she reassured.

He coated his dick and rubbed her starfish down. Sucking on his cheek, he pushed a finger into her tight ass, and she moaned. He fingered her, stretching her until two fingers slid in comfortably. She reached under herself, playing with her pussy once more. Another moan and she began rocking against his hand, encouraging him to be rougher, deeper, and more importantly, faster.

"You ready for this?" He gripped her hips, the tip of his cock pressing against her ass.

"Give it to me, Peter." She leaned back and the tip slid in, making her moan. "Fuck me until you come, please fuck me."

Swallowing, he pushed inside, slow, and gauging her every reaction. He didn't stop until their bodies pressed snug against one another. She was so tight, his cock throbbing in the heat of this unknown territory. Her fingers dipped into her pussy and she grinded against him, making him grunt.

"You're making me so wet," she whimpered.

His heart raced, her whimpering and pleading adding fuel to his fire. Licking his lips, he pulled out all the way and dove in a little faster. He repeated this, speeding up as they hummed and moaned in a dark language only

The Pied Piper's Pipe

they could understand. Curious as he began to fuck her gently, a hand slid over her hip and between her soaked thighs. She let him play with her hardened jewel and she dripped with each push.

"Good gravy, woman," he panted, his arousal cresting. His fingers dove inside her pussy as he fucked her ass. Every touch was breathtakingly erotic. "Did you just orgasm a second time?"

"Don't stop," she demanded. "Touch me more! Fuck me harder!"

His other hand slid to a breast, groping the soft ball of flesh before twisting her nipple. She tightened, both on his fingers and cock. It was like spurs to the horse and he took the opening. He thrusted hard into her. His orgasm peaked. With his cock stiff and hard, she wailed with a visceral scream, reverberating through the bar walls.

The pool table creaked as he leaned his weight into the last push, coming hard inside her. He had held on for so long, the aching release felt bittersweet. Peter sucked in air, stifling his own orgasmic scream. She rocked into his hand and dick, coming for a third time, cupping the hand over her breast as she hummed.

They froze, throbbing against each other as they gasped for air. Swallowing, Peter was the first to move, gently pulling his cock from her ass. She bit her lip, grabbing an ass cheek as his cum dribbled from it in a white stream. The site of it arousing and provocative, like his own personal porno.

If I could just have a picture of that view for those lonely nights. Mmm-mmm!

"You like what you see?" His eyes locked with hers, and he blushed. "The way you stare at my body...it make me feel—wanted."

The Pied Piper's Pipe

He let his eyes trailed the cum dripping from her pussy. "You're a wild one, Red."

"And you're a good lover." She wiggled her ass, letting more cum dripping out. "So, you still going to Canada?"

"Canada who?" Temptation called him but his cock returned to recovery mode and his busted knuckle aching. The promise of pleasure and sex made him ache, hoping the feeling to last forever.

Red laughed. "Exactly."

Reaching for her, he slid a thumb into her ass and hummed. "I'm not done working here."

"Oh?" There it was, that signature sound she had given him earlier in the day.

With his other hand, he slid two fingers into her pussy and began stroking her fast, firm against the sweet spot he'd discovered earlier. She squealed, gripping the edge of the table as he overwhelmed her. Again, an orgasm peaked, her pussy gushing with yet another climax. He didn't slow until her knees shook and at last, gave way. Catching her up in his arms, he smirked to see he had at last exhausted his wanton, red-headed woman.

"You got a shower in this place, woman?" He laughed, happy to have out lasted her.

"Through my office."

Epilogue

"Come on, Beau." Lou took a sip of beer, nudging his buddy on the left. "What happened to you last weekend? You missed a hell of a sex party! Tell him, Taylor."

Taylor choked on his shot. "Not so loud," he shushed him. "It was embarrassing enough you convinced me to wear that high school play mask."

"Wait." Beau gave a confused expression as his phone buzzed. "The troll mask?"

"Never mind that." Lou put the conversation back on track. "Come on, spill it. You got laid, but with who?"

"I don't know if I should say." Beau smirked, clearly texting someone.

"You boys need any refills?" Red stood with hands on hips, dressed in a crop top and daisy dukes.

"I'm buying these guys another shot, and maybe they'll speak up," Lou drawled, draining the last of his beer. "And I guess a bucket, it's gonna be a long night."

"Coming right up." She began to set up a bucket with ice, crushing bottles of Yuengling into it. "So, what have you boys been up to?"

She glanced up and flinched. Beau and Taylor averted their eyes with flushed faces. Lou on the other hand had a look of pure mischief and screamed, *I got laid, how about you?* She laughed, shaking her head as she shoved the bucket of beers to him. Pulling out two shot glasses she glared at the two shy college boys.

"So, what will it be?" she cooed, enjoying the moment. "You gonna tell me or am I guessing?"

"Taylor! Beau!" Lou smacked their shoulders on either side of him. "Answer the lady."

"I fucked my high school crush at an orgy party," Taylor blurted.

Red blinked, and Peter froze behind him with a face that said, *did I just hear that right?*

Feeling the pressure of Peter, Beau confessed, "I fucked my professor."

Both college kids stared at her, everything about their posture and faces filled with dread as if reporting in against their will. Red laughed until tears shone in her eyes. Peter roared behind them, gasping for air as he patted both of them on the back.

"I was asking about what shot you wanted." Red chuckled. "In fact, that was worth a free shot for you both. Name it."

"Give them some Sambuca." Peter reached between them, grabbing a glass of water that was prepped for him. "They may not want to remember tonight after that one."

With that, Peter left, and Red returned to her customers, sliding shots across the counter. "Sounds like we all got lucky then."

Lou popped open his next drink. "I bet you went to that sex party in the 'burbs too."

Her eyebrows arched. "Yeah, like most of the town."

"I'll have to put in a formal complaint." Lou had a sparkle in his eye, a toothy grin on his face. "Since when did you start wearing bras?"

She nodded, licking her teeth. "Since I needed a way to slow down my man over there."

The three of them spun, and Peter waved. "He gets rather jealous if anyone stares at them for too long."

She leaned on the counter, her cleavage threatening to escape her red lacy bra.

The Troll, the Wolf, and Beau paled.

THE END

Honey Cummings

A passionate, award-winning author of Fantasy, Honey has turned her aim towards erotica. Blending everyday scenarios and crafting them into steamy, blood-boiling moments for every shade of audience. Whether you want something short and hot like a student-teacher hook up to the more paranormal flair where Sleep with Sasquatch has unexpected bonus, look forward to erotic short stories, novellas, and hopefully a Trilogy in the future. Honey's debut erotic short landed No. 3 in Urban Erotica and continues to satisfy readers time and time again. Be sure to leave her a review and let her know what you think!

https://www.amazon.com/Honey-Cummings/e/B07WFX5FDX

www.AuthorHoneyCummings.com

instagram.com/authorhoneycummings

twitter.com/HoneyCummings2

facebook.com/Author-Honey-Cummings-101408818012749

Honey Cummings

More Honey Cummings Books

Sleeping with Sasquatch

Cuddling with Chupacabra

Naked with New Jersey Devil

Laying with the Lady in Blue

Wanton Woman in White

Beating it with Bloody Mary

Beau and Professor Bestialora

The Goat's Gruff

Goldie and Her Three Beards

Pied Piper's Pipe

Princess Pea's Bed

Jack's Beanstalk

The Pied Piper's Pipe

4 Horsemen Publications

Erotica

Dalia Lance

My Home on Whore Island

Slumming It on Slut Street

Training of the Tramp

72% Match

Ali Whippe

Office Hours

Tutoring Center

Athletics

Extra Credit

Honey Cummings

Fantasy/Paranormal Romance

Valerie Willis

Cedric the Demonic Knight

Romasanta: Father of Werewolves

The Oracle: Keeper of the Gaea's Gate

Artemis: Eye of Gaea

King Incubus: A New Reign

J.M. Paquette

Klauden's Ring

Solyn's Body

Hannah's Heart

4HorsemenPublications.com

www.ingramcontent.com/pod-product-compliance
Lightning Source LLC
LaVergne TN
LVHW091934070526
838200LV00068B/1053